SADDLEBACK
PUBLISHING·INC.

Barclay
Family
Adventures

THE Pass

BY

Ed Hanson

THE BARCLAY FAMILY ADVENTURES

Development and Production: Laurel Associates, Inc.
Cover and Interior Art: Black Eagle Productions

SADDLEBACK
PUBLISHING·INC.
Three Watson
Irvine, CA 92618-2767
E-Mail: info@sdlback.com
Website: www.sdlback.com

ISBN 1-56254-557-4

Printed in the United States of America
08 07 06 05 04   9 8 7 6 5 4 3 2 1

CONTENTS

MEET THE BARCLAYS

Paul Barclay
A fun-loving father of three who takes his kids on his travels whenever he can.

Ann Barclay
The devoted mother who manages the homefront during Paul's many absences as an on-site construction engineer.

Jim Barclay
The eldest child, Jim is a talented athlete with his eye on a football scholarship at a major college.

Aaron Barclay
Three years younger than Jim, he's inquisitive, daring, and an absolute whiz in science class.

Pam Barclay
Adopted from Korea as a baby, Pam is a spunky middle-schooler who more than holds her own with her lively older brothers.

CHAPTER 1

Getting Ready

Jim Barclay jogged off the field toward the locker room. Coach Brocko had worked the team hard today. Jim's jersey was soaked in sweat, and he was looking forward to a hot shower.

At almost 18, Jim was a high school senior this year. The weight workouts he'd begun as a sophomore were really paying off. Back then, Jim had weighed 180 pounds and was bench pressing about 210 pounds.

By his junior year, Jim's weight was up to 210 pounds and he was benching 290. And now he stood 6 feet 2 inches tall and weighed a rock-hard 225. He was bench pressing some 340 pounds of iron.

In his junior year, Jim had made the

first string All-State team in both offense and defense. He was the first player in more than 15 years to do that. An outstanding running back, he had unusual quickness and speed as well as the power to run over most opponents.

But some sportswriters and coaches thought Jim was an even better defensive player. As a left linebacker, he controlled half the line of scrimmage. That allowed his teammates to concentrate on the other half, giving the Rockdale Rams an excellent defense.

The first game was only a week away. The sportswriters were expecting a great season from Jim Barclay and the Rams team. Last year they'd won eight games and lost two. Many were predicting an undefeated season this year. For the first time ever, the Rams had a good chance to win the state championship.

Jim's younger brother Aaron was entering his freshman year of high school. Although he weighed only 145 pounds, he had tried out for the football team.

Football wasn't his favorite sport, but Aaron admired his older brother and wanted to follow in his footsteps. Aaron was surprised to make Coach Brocko's final cut. He was a third-string defensive back and wide receiver.

Jim's muscles ached from the long practice, and the hot water felt good. He thought about the coming season. Would the Rams go undefeated? Would he make All State again? Only time would tell.

After getting dressed, Jim yelled out to Aaron. "Hurry up, Aaron, and I'll give you a ride home."

Aaron was ready to go. He grabbed his gym bag and followed his brother out to the car.

"Do you know what Mom's cooking for dinner tonight?" Jim asked.

"Spaghetti and meatballs, I think," Aaron answered.

"Good! I'm so hungry I could eat a horse," Jim said.

Aaron laughed. "So what else is new? Most of the time you eat enough for *three* normal people."

Jim reached over and gave Aaron a playful tap on the head. "Maybe if *you'd* eat more you wouldn't be such a little shrimp," he teased.

"Well, I don't need to be big. I've got a superior brain," Aaron added with a laugh.

Jim smiled. Ten minutes later, he pulled into their driveway.

"Hi, Mom!" they both yelled as they walked into the kitchen.

Ann Barclay was busy at the stove. "How was practice?" she asked as she stirred a big pot of spaghetti sauce.

Jim winked at his mother. "It was okay—except Aaron keeps trying to hurt me," he teased. Then he grabbed a spoon and began to sample the sauce.

Pretending to be annoyed, Ann pushed them both away. "I'll call you when supper is ready," she said. "Go find something productive to do until then."

The two hungry boys went into the living room where their younger sister Pam was reading.

"So, how are the two football heroes?" she asked in a mocking voice.

Aaron was quick to answer. "Oh, *I'm* okay, Pam. But I'm not sure how the big oaf is doing. I had to push him around quite a bit at practice today."

Pam giggled. "Oh, sure—*that'll* be the day," she said.

Jim smiled at their joking and picked up the evening paper. A story about the upcoming football season was right on the front page.

CHAPTER 2

Season Opener

Paul Barclay sat in an office about a thousand miles away from Rockdale. He was trying to convince his boss to give him weekends off for the next three months.

"Paul, there's just no way we can do that," said Ed Badger, the state supervisor. "That bridge has to be finished by spring. We'll be needing you on Saturdays to supervise the work."

"But, Ed, you don't understand!" Paul pleaded. "This is my son's last year of high school. He's one of the best football players in the state. I've just *got* to be there for his games."

Ed Badger thought about it for a moment. He knew that Barclay was one of the top construction engineers in the whole country. He certainly didn't want to lose him.

Finally, he said, "I'll tell you what we can do. We'll give you every other weekend off. That way, you can see half the games."

Now it was Paul's turn to ponder. His work always meant major commitments of time away from his family.

"Okay, it's a deal, then. But I'll need to have this weekend off so I can see the opening game."

"Done," Ed Badger said with a smile.

That evening, Paul called his ex-wife. When he told her he'd be in town for Saturday's game, she was delighted. She offered to pick him up at the airport and take him to the stadium. She knew how happy Jim would be that his dad would be able to attend the game.

Coach Brocko had canceled practice for the two days before the opener. He'd worked the team hard in August. He knew they were in great shape and ready to play football. The coach was a bit worried about his star player, however.

This year, the pressure on Jim Barclay was going to be unbelievable. Several sportswriters were predicting that Jim would break every rushing record in the state's history.

Then there were all the college recruiters! The coach would try to protect Jim from them as best he could. But Jim was so well-known that it would be difficult. How would he handle the pressure and the publicity?

On Friday the sports page headline read:

ROCKDALE RAMS
OPEN SEASON TOMORROW
Favored by 20 Points Over Cassville

Jim sat in the locker room next to Tony Moore. His best friend on the team, Tony was the starting right tackle. He was also the biggest and strongest player on the Rams team. Tony weighed 285 pounds and could bench press 400 pounds. He and Jim were both top college prospects.

Jim was a big fellow, but he always felt small sitting next to Tony. He looked at his friend and said, "Are you going to open a few holes for me today? Or will I have to do everything myself?"

Tony laughed. "You know I do all the hard work, and you get all the publicity," he answered. "Life isn't fair."

Just then Coach Brocko called the team together. "Gentlemen," he said, "today we start a new season. Many people are predicting great things for the Rams this year. But all I ask of you is just one thing—*do your very best.*

"If you do your very best and we lose—you and I have nothing to be ashamed of."

With that, they headed onto the field for the first game of the season.

Cassville won the coin toss and elected to receive. They made four yards on three running plays and punted. Billy Zitto, a shifty Rams return man, took the punt at his 40-yard line. He ran it back to midfield.

On the first play from scrimmage, Jim Barclay broke over the right tackle. He mowed down two Cassville defenders. Then he carried two more players with him into the end zone for a touchdown.

As Jim ran back to the bench, Tony Moore yelled, "That hole was so big my *grandmother* could have scored!"

Jim laughed—as did several other teammates. Everyone was used to the good-natured kidding that went on between these two good friends.

Cassville made a first down on its second possession. Now they were on their own 35-yard line with six yards to go. As their quarterback went back to pass, Jim came charging in. He hit the quarterback just before he could get the pass off. Then, when the ball bounced off the ground, Jim scooped it up. In a flash, he ran into the end zone for his second touchdown of the game!

Back on the bench, Jim looked over at Tony. "Hey, buddy! You didn't help me much on *that* play," he said with a big grin.

Now it was Cassville's turn to receive. In a few minutes, they were forced to punt. Four plays later, Jim went around left-end for his third touchdown.

Coach Brocko had seen enough. It was still the first quarter, and the score was 21 to 0. He replaced Jim on offense with Billy Zitto. Jim played the rest of the game on defense and never again touched the football.

The next day the papers read:

CASSVILLE NO MATCH FOR RAMS
Final Score, 42–0
Jim Barclay Scores 3 TDs

CHAPTER 3

The Test

Game two was more of the same. Oakmore was a smaller school than Rockdale High. Their coach had fewer players to draw on. The lopsided score was 47–0. Again, Coach Brocko took his starting players out of the game early.

Everyone was excited about the third game. Springfield had also won its first two games. The players were said to be big and physical. At last a real test was coming up for the Rockdale Rams!

The game was to be held in Springfield. The trip was a 40-mile bus ride.

Paul Barclay had arrived in Springfield the morning of the game. After Paul met Ann and Pam at the gate, they took their seats in the stands. Excitement was in the air. The home team fans were wondering just how good Rockdale really was. This game should help answer that question.

Several college scouts had come to watch Jim Barclay and Tony Moore. And Springfield also had several players the colleges were considering. The hottest prospect was Marc Richman, a tall quarterback with a strong arm.

According to Coach Brocko, keeping heavy pressure on Richman was the key to winning this game.

"If you guys give him all day to throw, he'll kill us," the coach had said.

Springfield won the coin toss and elected to receive. They took the opening kickoff up to the 38-yard line.

On the first play from scrimmage, Richman completed a 22-yard pass. Now the ball was on the Rams' 40-yard line. The next time Richman faded back to pass, Jim shot forward. He was met forcefully by the big fullback and a 260-pound tackle.

The two players had hit Jim just right.

He found himself on his back! Again the pass was complete—this time to the 25-yard line. *Coach was right*, Jim thought to himself. *If our defense can't sack this guy, he'll pick us apart.*

Two running plays gained seven yards. It was now third down. Springfield was on the 18-yard line with three yards to go for a first down.

Richman took the ball from the center and faked to his fullback. When most of the Rams team went for the fullback, he lofted a soft pass to a receiver in the end zone. The extra point was good. The score was 7–0.

Coach Brocko pulled his defense together on the sideline. "Put more pressure on the quarterback! Jim, I know they're double-teaming you, but you've *got* to get to him!"

"I know that, Coach," Jim answered.

Springfield kicked off and Billy Zitto ran it back to the 41-yard line. Rockdale's offense was determined. They made three first downs and brought the ball to Springfield's 11-yard line. On the next play, Jim faked into the line. Then he cut outside and scored without even being touched! Rockdale's ace kicker easily made the extra point.

The game then settled into a defensive battle. Rockdale was pouring pressure on the quarterback. Richman was very frustrated. With less time to throw, he was missing his receivers. But the Springfield defense was holding the Rams in check as well. When Jim failed to make a first down by just one yard, the Rams punted for the third time. At halftime, the score was still tied at 7–7.

In the locker room, Jim sat next to Tony Moore.

"I guess we have our work cut out for us," Tony said.

"Yeah," Jim agreed. "But they don't seem to be hitting me as hard as they did at the beginning of the game. Maybe they're getting tired."

After the coach's pep talk, the Rams took the field for the second half. Now they were fired up and ready to go.

This time, Rockdale received the kickoff. Four plays later, Jim rumbled 52 yards for his second TD. He'd followed Tony through a gaping hole in the line.

Back on the bench, Jim said, "Why didn't you do that in the first half, Tony?"

"I did," the big lineman yelled back. "You just kept missing the hole."

Rockdale dominated the rest of the game. Late in the fourth quarter, the Rams were ahead, 28–7, when Springfield completed a long pass for a touchdown. The final score was 28–14, in favor of the Rams.

As the Barclays were leaving the stadium, Paul squeezed Ann's arm.

"Your son played a heck of a game today," he said.

"He sure did," she agreed. "You know, Paul—the house won't be the same with Jim gone next year."

"I know. But maybe he'll pick a college nearby and come home often."

"I sure hope so. I'm going to miss him a lot," Ann said.

Paul put his arms around Pam and her mother as they walked to the car.

CHAPTER 4

The Plot

The next day the headline read:

RAMS FOR REAL—
SPRINGFIELD GOES DOWN, 28–14

Jim Barclay continues his attack on the state rushing record. Yesterday he rushed for 212 yards and scored four touchdowns. As usual, Tony Moore was a major force on the line. Some college scouts are now calling him the best offensive lineman in the east.

The next three games were easy victories for the Rams. Now they had six wins, and the pressure was building for a perfect season.

But a debate was raging in Rockdale. Some people were finding fault with

Coach Brocko. They criticized him for putting Jim on the sidelines whenever the team had a big lead.

One local sportswriter wrote:

> *Coach Brocko hinders Barclay's chances to break the state rushing record! Jim Barclay is playing only half of most games. How can he set a new record at this pace?*

Coach Brocko defended himself. "Setting records is not our goal," he said. "Winning the state championship is our number one priority—along with keeping our players healthy. We're not interested in embarrassing other teams by running up the score."

Should Jim Barclay continue to play when the game was already won? The local newspaper asked its readers to vote on the issue. When the results of the survey were totaled, most sport fans agreed with the coach. No record was worth running up 60–0 scores. The survey put an end to the debate.

*   *   *

Two men were shooting pool in a seedy Rockdale neighborhood. Dooley's poolroom was not a place for the timid. The police were often called there to break up fights or make an arrest.

Dooley's was the place to go if you wanted drugs or a stolen car. In fact, there wasn't much trouble that you *couldn't* find at Dooley's!

The bigger of the two pool players weighed about 260 pounds. About 20 years earlier, he'd been an impressive, muscular man. Now, he was 40 pounds overweight and badly out of shape.

The big fellow looked like an old heavyweight boxer who'd gone to seed. And yet, Big Louie, as he was known, was still a person to be avoided. He rarely lost a barroom fight—and there had been many of them!

A skinny man with deep sunken eyes lined up his shot. "Six ball, side pocket," he barked. This was Louie's friend, Wes Hawes—known all over town as "Snake."

Wes actually *looked* like his nickname. He was sneaky, dangerous, and just as unpredictable as a rattlesnake.

As the six ball dropped into the pocket, Louie said, "I think there's a good chance that Rockdale will play for the state championship. This town will go crazy, Snake. The Rams would be the first team in history to play for the state title."

"So what?" Snake muttered as he sank two more balls.

"Well, I was just thinking—what if we took steps to make sure Rockdale *can't* win? What if we bet a bundle on their opponent?"

Snake was interested. "And just how are we going to do that?" he asked.

"By taking their star player out of the game," Louie replied.

Snake laughed. "You know, Louie, you may have a good idea there."

CHAPTER 5

The Fight

Jim had been dating Peggy Turner for two years. They got along great! Tonight he and Peggy were going to a dance in town.

Jim had his arm around Peggy as they walked in. Waving to several friends, he escorted Peggy to a table at the far end of the room. Then a guy Jim had never seen before approached their table. He walked with a cocky swagger as if he was very sure of himself.

As Peggy and Jim looked up, he said to her, "Let's dance, baby."

"No, thanks," Peggy said politely as she turned her attention back to Jim.

"Come on—don't be so stuck up," the stranger insisted. When she didn't respond, he grabbed Peggy's wrist and started pulling her to her feet.

Jim bolted out of his chair and grasped the guy's arm in an iron grip.

"The lady said *no*," Jim said quietly. "I think you'd better leave now."

The stranger winced in pain. He glared at Jim and said, "Okay, okay! But I won't forget this!" Jim let go of his arm, and the scowling intruder walked away.

Soon Peggy and Jim had forgotten the whole incident. After dancing awhile, they sat and talked. They were so involved in their conversation they didn't see Tony Moore come up to their table.

"How're you doing, hotshot?" Tony said with a grin.

"I'd be better if you knew how to block," Jim replied. They both laughed.

"Jim, did you have a run-in with a guy about an hour ago?"

"Nothing serious, Tony. Some doofus asked Peggy to dance. He had a little trouble taking no for an answer," Jim replied.

"Well, old buddy, that guy's a member of the Skull gang. He and five of his friends seem to be looking for trouble."

"Come on! You know that I'm not going to bother anybody," Jim said.

"Yeah, I know that. But there's no guarantee that they won't bother *you*. I think I'll stick around, just in case you need a little help."

"Hey, I can take care of myself," Jim protested.

"You can do okay—but not against six guys. Besides, maybe Peggy will see what a great guy I am and give me a chance."

"Great," said Jim. "Now I've got a 285-pound babysitter!"

Jim and Peggy danced a few more times. About 11 o'clock they headed for the door. Jim's car was parked a block or so away. But as Jim and Peggy walked around the corner, the sidewalk was suddenly blocked by six guys.

The stranger who'd asked Peggy to dance snarled at Jim.

"What do you want?" Jim said calmly.

"Maybe we want to see how tough a big football star like you really is."

Then a voice from behind Jim spoke up. "Well, *I'm* a football star, too—and I think the two of us can wipe up the floor with you bums."

Tony stepped out of the shadows. *I love Tony,* Jim thought to himself, *but he sure doesn't believe in negotiation. Heck, I'm on a date—I don't want to get into a fight now!*

Jim gave Peggy the car keys. "Get in the car and lock the doors. And don't open them for anyone but Tony or me."

All six gang members charged in. Tony grabbed the first two and slammed their heads together. Both dropped to the sidewalk. Then Jim caught the guy who'd asked Peggy to dance and landed a hard punch on his cheekbone. Letting out a cry of pain, the guy fell to the pavement.

Jim turned to see Tony struggling with the other three. He pulled one of the men off of his friend and hit him solidly in the pit of his stomach. The man doubled over, gasping for air.

The last two attackers decided that they'd jumped the wrong people. They turned around and took off running. As Tony and Jim approached the car, Peggy opened the door and jumped out. She looked frightened and upset.

"Are you both okay?" she asked.

"We're fine," Jim answered. "But I'm not sure about those guys."

The four Skulls were still struggling to get to their feet.

"Hop in, Tony. I'll drop you off before I take Peggy home."

"Whatever you say, hotshot. I guess that's enough excitement for one day," Tony said with a grin.

CHAPTER 6

An Angry Coach

At practice the next day, both Jim and Tony took a lot of teasing from their teammates. Jim had a big bruise on his left cheek and a cut over his right eye. Tony's black eye was turning blacker by the minute. Their teammates laughed, but Coach Brocko saw nothing funny about it.

"What's the matter with you two idiots?" he yelled. "We have a chance at the state championship. What if you'd been seriously hurt? Do you guys want to blow your college scholarships? Why has God given me such a bunch of morons to coach?" he moaned.

Jim and Tony listened silently as the coach chewed them out. They wanted to explain that it wasn't their fault, but they

31

knew that any excuse was hopeless.

Finally, Coach Brocko ordered the team onto the field. As they were heading out of the locker room, Jim and Tony heard him say, "Don't plan on getting home early. You guys are going to be doing extra laps tonight!"

And Coach Brocko kept his word. It was dark outside when Jim and Tony jogged in from the track for a shower.

"The next fight you guys get in will cost you eight miles!" the coach shouted before he left.

Back at home, Pam was talking to her mother in the kitchen.

"Mom," she said, "I've suddenly become very popular—especially with the girls. But all they do is ask me questions about my big brother."

"Well, dear, that's normal. Your brother is sort of a hero in this town now—and young girls like a hero."

"But, Mom!" Pam complained. "I want people to like me for *me*, not for my big brother, the star football player."

"Of course you do, Pam. But remember that Jim will be away at college next year. When he's gone, you'll miss him."

"I know, Mom," Pam sighed. "He's been a great brother."

Aaron arrived home about 5 o'clock. He was alone when he walked in.

"Where's your brother?" Ann asked.

"Coach ordered Jim and Tony to run four extra miles on the track. He should be home about 6 o'clock."

At ten minutes past six, Jim straggled in the back door. Ann frowned at him.

"Well, maybe you'll think twice about getting into another fight," she said.

"*I* didn't start the fight, Mom. I was attacked! Why can't I get that point across?" Jim groaned.

* * *

The last four games of the season ended in Rockdale victories. The Rams finished the season with 10 wins and no losses. It wasn't important that Jim hadn't broken the rushing record. Everyone knew that he could have done it easily if he'd played full games all season.

Several colleges were eager to get Jim into their programs. The scouts' interest in Tony was almost as strong.

Tony and Jim had talked about what fun it would be to go to the same school.

"Wouldn't it be great if we could play four more years together?" Tony said.

"Yeah, that would be the best, Tony. Let's hope it happens. But right now, we'd better focus on Morgantown."

CHAPTER 7

A New Beginning

The next day's newspaper headline read:

**RAMS GO UNDEFEATED!
ROCKDALE TO PLAY MORGANTOWN
FOR THE STATE CHAMPIONSHIP**

On paper, Rockdale didn't appear to have much of a chance against mighty Morgantown. Rockdale High had only 800 students, compared to more than 4,000 at Morgantown.

Morgantown was the defending state champ. The Rams had never played in a state championship game. They'd gone undefeated this year, but many felt that Morgantown's schedule had been much tougher.

Rockdale, of course, had Jim Barclay. But Morgantown had a more balanced team. Their huge line outweighed the Rams by 35 pounds per man. They also had a solid running game and an equally good passing attack.

Just before game day, the sportswriters had made Morgantown a seven-point favorite.

The game would be played on a neutral field—the big stadium at State College in Springfield.

*   *   *

Paul Barclay had been rethinking his life. He was getting tired of the constant travel. He still loved Ann and missed being with her and the kids. *Maybe it's time to give up this job*, he thought to himself. *Maybe Ann and I should try and get back together.*

Years ago, Paul had been recruited to fill an opening in the engineering department at State College. Ann had urged him to take it, but he had refused. Perhaps now was the time. It was only a

40-mile drive from Rockdale to Springfield—an easy enough commute. He wouldn't make nearly as much money teaching, but that didn't seem so important now.

Without telling anyone, Paul had come to Springfield the day before. He'd arranged an interview with the head of the engineering department.

The interview had gone well; Paul knew the job was his if he wanted it. But, of course, he couldn't start until his current construction project was finished.

After the interview, he called Ann. "How about having dinner tonight?"

"Shall I invite the kids?" Ann asked.

"No, Ann, not this time. I want to talk with you alone."

After dinner, Paul expressed his hopes that they might get back together. He told her about his interview and the new job possibility.

"It would mean an end to all the traveling, Ann. No more being away half the year. I'd be home all the time. I think that's what you've always wanted."

Ann was stunned. She had no idea that Paul was thinking this way.

Then Paul added, "Of course, I'll be earning less money—"

Ann interrupted him. "That's not important," she said, squeezing his hand. "I've always told you that."

CHAPTER 8

The Abduction

At 4 o'clock on Friday afternoon, Ann asked Jim to run a couple of errands for her. "I'd go myself, Jim, but your dad will be here soon. I want to have a nice dinner ready for him."

"Sure, Mom. No problem," Jim replied. He hopped in the car and headed toward the mall. He found a space at the far end of the parking lot.

When he opened the door, a black van pulled up right alongside him. Paying no attention, Jim got out and closed his door. Then, he felt something poking at his ribs! A deep voice behind him said, "Kid, this is a nine-millimeter handgun. If you don't want to get hurt, you'll do as I say."

Jim thought about his options. He was

young and strong—but with a gun in his ribs, there was little he could do.

"What do you want?" he asked.

"Get in the van—now."

Two more men were inside the van—the driver who never said a word and a skinny man with deep sunken eyes.

As the black van drove away, the skinny man smirked at Jim. When he spoke, his voice was cold and mean.

"You aren't such a big football star now, are you?" he said in a mocking voice. Jim didn't answer. "So what do you think? Who's going to win the big game now that *you* won't be playing?"

Jim wanted to get his hands around the skinny man's neck, but he knew that was impossible.

They drove for half an hour or so before stopping. Then, while keeping the pistol aimed at Jim's chest, the big man ordered him out of the van.

Trying to get his bearings, Jim looked around. He wasn't sure where he was, but it looked like it might be an old junkyard.

An old trailer truck was in the corner of the yard. Two of the men forced Jim inside and bound his hands behind his back. Then they tied his feet together.

Before Jim's captors left the truck, the skinny man turned to him.

"Goodbye, football hero," he sneered.

A moment later, Jim heard the sound of a padlock closing on the rear doors.

Jim calculated his chances. He realized they had no intention of releasing him. He could easily identify both of them. But getting to the football game was the least of his concerns at the moment. Staying alive was number one!

It wasn't easy to move with his hands and feet tied. Jim awkwardly inched his way around the trailer, hoping to find something to help him. Finally, he found a small piece of glass. *This is probably from a broken bottle,* he thought to himself. *Maybe I can use it to cut the rope!*

But the piece of glass had no sharp

edge! After Jim rubbed the rope for 10 minutes, it was still intact. Now he wondered what time it was. He couldn't see his watch, but he figured it must be about midnight.

*   *   *

Jim's mother was concerned when he didn't get back in time for supper. When Paul arrived, he told Ann not to worry. "He probably ran into some friends, Ann. They got talking about tomorrow's big game and lost track of the time."

Ann wasn't convinced. "Maybe you're right—but Jim always calls when he's going to be late," she said with a frown.

At 11 o'clock, there was still no sign of Jim. Paul called Coach Brocko.

"Coach, this is Paul Barclay calling. I'm sorry to bother you so late, but Jim hasn't come home. I was wondering if you might know where he is."

The coach was worried. "Gee, I don't know, Mr. Barclay. Let me make a few calls," he answered.

Coach Brocko called back in about 10 minutes. No one had seen Jim. Ann was feeling really alarmed now. She started to cry, and Paul called the police.

It was 2 o'clock in the morning when the police found Jim's car in the parking lot. The officers figured that all the evidence pointed to some kind of kidnapping.

Paul did his best to comfort Ann. "Please don't worry, dear. The police will find him. Everything will be all right—you'll see!"

*   *   *

Far across town, Jim was still inching his way around the van in the dark. He couldn't see anything, so he had to rely on his sense of touch.

At last he had a little luck. He found some more pieces of broken glass. He ran his finger along several pieces until he found one that seemed sharp.

Working strictly from feel, he started rubbing the sharp edge against the rope. It was hard work. Every few minutes, Jim's hand would cramp up, and he'd have to stop and rest.

Finally, he cut through the rope around his wrists! With his hands free, he quickly untied his legs. *Well, I'm free of the ropes,* Jim thought to himself. *But how am I going to get out of this truck?*

Jim looked around desperately. He could see some thin rays of light coming into the truck's side panel. He looked at his watch again. The game was only six hours away!

Four heavy wooden pallets were stacked in the far corner of the truck. Jim figured that each one weighed about 40 pounds. He picked one up and walked over to the crack in the panel wall. *Maybe this is a weak point,* he thought to himself.

Then Jim lifted the pallet and started to use it as a battering ram! Again and again he pounded the heavy pallet against the truck wall. Gradually, parts of the panel crumpled. Finally, he'd punched a jagged hole that was big enough to poke his head through.

Jim continued to pound at the hole with the pallet. At last, the opening was big enough for him to crawl through! He looked at his watch. It was five minutes to eleven! His heart fell. The team was already in Springfield, getting dressed for the big game.

CHAPTER 9

A Rush to the Stadium

Jim tumbled out of the truck. He started to run down the rural road at a fast pace. After about a mile, he came to a small country store. As he ran in the door, he yelled, "I'm Jim Barclay. I've been kidnapped. Call the police."

Old man Briggs knew Jim the minute he saw him. Briggs was a football fan, and Jim's picture had been in the local paper all season. Even before Jim finished talking, Briggs was dialing the police.

Jim grabbed the phone. "Will you try to get me to the game in Springfield? I'm at Briggs's store on the outskirts of town."

"We'll do our best, son. How about we

get you there in a state police helicopter? You just stay put, young fella. We'll get a car to you in no time."

Jim called home next. He told his parents what had happened and assured them that he was all right.

"The police are trying to get hold of a helicopter to take me to the game," he added.

"Are you sure you're okay?" Ann asked.

"I'm fine, Mom—but I just *have* to get to the game. Please understand."

"We understand, son. We'll be listening on the radio."

A few minutes later, a Rockdale police car pulled up. "Hop in, Jim. The state 'copter will be waiting at the airport."

On the way to the airport, Jim told the officers about his abduction. After he described the men who grabbed him, one of the officers spoke up. "I think I know those guys. It sounds like Big Louie and Snake. They like to bet real heavy, and they *don't* like to lose!"

Then the officer called the station. An immediate order was issued to pick up the two suspects.

"And do *not* release any information whatsoever about Jim Barclay," the officer warned. "Not until we have those two rats trapped in a cell."

* * *

Big Louie and Snake walked into Dooley's. It was just a few minutes before game time. As they grabbed a couple of cues, Louie said to Dooley, "Get the football game on the radio."

"Okay," Dooley said. "It probably won't be much of a game, though. I heard that Rockdale's star running back is missing."

Snake grinned. "Yeah, I heard that, too. Ain't it a shame?"

At the end of the first quarter, Louie and Snake were all smiles. Morgantown was ahead, 10–0.

"I think we made ourselves a cool 10 grand today," Snake bragged.

"Well, just remember whose idea it was," Louie answered.

At that moment, two police cars pulled up outside Dooley's door. There were six officers inside the cars. Two of them went around to the back of the pool hall. The other four walked in the front door.

Louie and Snake were sitting at a table in the far corner of the room. Snake saw the officers first. He didn't think much about it—the police were always at Dooley's. But when they started to come his way, Snake got concerned.

"You're under arrest," was all the first officer said.

"Huh? What for?" Louie protested.

"You know what for. Now move it."

Once Jim's kidnappers were in custody, word of Jim's escape quickly went out.

Halfway through the second quarter, an announcement blared out over the stadium loudspeaker:

Ladies and Gentlemen—Jim Barclay has been found, and he is safe! He just arrived at the stadium, in fact. He should be reporting to the field within minutes.

The roar of relief from the stands was deafening. Even the Morgantown fans stood up and cheered.

When Jim ran onto the field, there were four minutes left to play in the first half. At the sight of him, the crowd again went wild. The score was now 17–0 in favor of Morgantown.

With two minutes left in the half, the Rams took over on their own 30-yard line. On the first play, they faked to Jim and handed off to Billy Zitto. The whole Mules team went for the fake! Billy scampered 22 yards for a first down.

On the next play Jim took the handoff and followed Tony Moore through the line. Tony leveled the defensive lineman, and Jim ran over the linebacker.

Two defensive backs hit him hard at the 10-yard line—but they couldn't tackle him! He dragged the two players into the end zone for Rockdale's first score!

The half ended with the Rockdale Rams trailing, 17–7. In the locker room, Coach Brocko had trouble getting the team's attention. Everyone was eager to hear all the details of Jim's kidnapping.

Finally, the coach shouted, "Listen up, guys! We have a football game to win. Let's concentrate on that. Jim can tell us his story later."

CHAPTER 10

The Last Half

Coach Brocko was worried. Due to injuries, four of his starting players couldn't play the second half. The Morgantown Mules were very rough. Coach wondered if he'd have 11 healthy players left to finish the game.

Morgantown took the second half kick-off to the 40-yard line. On the next play, the Rams' starting tackle sprained his ankle. Coach Brocko searched his bench as the injured tackle limped over to the sideline. Just as he'd feared, the Rams were running out of players!

"Tony!" Coach called out. "How about playing some defense?"

Tony Moore was a great offensive tackle, but he'd never played defense!

"Sure," Tony said, grabbing his helmet.

As he trotted onto the field, Jim looked at his teammates. "Coach must be getting hard up. He's sending Tony in to play D."

Hearing his friend's remark, Tony said, "Coach sent me in to teach those guys how to tackle."

Two plays later, with the ball close to midfield, the Mules punted.

Rockdale ripped off three first downs. Jim was gaining six to seven yards per carry. But when the ball was on Morgantown's 35-yard line, the handoff was bobbled! The ball bounced on the ground and was quickly recovered by Morgantown.

* * *

Back in Rockdale, Paul and Ann were listening to the radio intently. When the Rams lost the fumble, Paul groaned, "This doesn't look too good!"

"But we still have a whole quarter to play," she said.

"I know, Ann, but it sounds like

we're about to run out of players."

The rest of the third quarter was a defensive struggle. Neither offensive team could get anything going.

But Rockdale got a lucky break early in the fourth quarter. The Mules fumbled and lost the ball on their own 20-yard line. Rockdale couldn't make a first down, but their kicker managed a short field goal. Now the score was 17–10.

Nothing changed as the fourth quarter dragged on. It seemed that neither team would score again. The game was still a defensive battle.

In the stands, an eerie silence fell over the Rockdale fans. Their team was now struggling to make a first down.

Half the starting lineup was injured and on the bench. There were only a few minutes left in the game. The Rams' prospects for a state championship were growing dim.

There were just 50 seconds left in the game when the Rams took their final possession. On the first play, Jim gained four yards. On second down, the Rockdale quarterback completed a nine-yard pass to Billy Zitto for another first down.

Jim and Tony dug in. They were absolutely determined to score. On the next play, Jim burst through another big hole made by his friend. Cutting to the sidelines, he outraced all the defenders into the end zone. But the timing was too close for comfort. There were just two seconds left in the game!

The announcer was so excited he could hardly go on calling the game.

"The score is 17–16," he kept yelling into the microphone. "It looks like this game may go into overtime."

The Rams team huddled on the side line. "Normally," Coach Brocko said, "I'd say kick the extra point and try to win in overtime. But today is different. We're all beat up. I think we have to go for two points and win this thing right now.

"But I don't know if you can get into

the end zone, Jim. Every Morgantown player will be after you as soon as you touch the ball. Let's fake a run wide and toss a short pass. What do you say? Do you think you can do that, Jim?"

"I'll try," Jim replied.

"It just might work, Jim. You haven't thrown a pass all season and they'll never be expecting it."

The two teams lined up for what would be the final play of the game. No place kicker had been put in the game. Again, the announcer had trouble controlling his voice. "The Rockdale Rams are going for a two-point conversion! I can't believe it! What a finish!"

The ball was snapped. Jim got the handoff and headed wide to his right. As expected, 11 Mules players were in hot pursuit. But just before he was buried in a mountain of blue uniforms, Jim lofted a soft pass over their outstretched hands.

In the press box, the announcer yelled, "Hold onto your hats, folks. It's a fake run.

It's a fake run! It's a pass! It's a pass!

"There's a Rams player all alone in the back of the end zone. There isn't a Morgantown Mule within ten yards of him! The intended receiver is Number 21—I'm not sure who it is."

Back in Rockdale, Paul jumped up off the couch. He was so excited he knocked over a lamp. "Did you hear that, Ann—Number 21—that's Aaron's number! Can you believe this? *The pass is to Aaron!*"

Aaron watched the football floating down toward him. He snatched the ball and hugged it to his chest. The referee raised his arms.

The game was over. The final score was Rockdale 18, Morgantown 17.

There wasn't a person on the Rams side of the field who wasn't screaming.

In their living room, Paul and Ann were jumping up and down and cheering. Jim was still buried under a pile of players. He had no idea what had happened.

When he saw Aaron riding on the

Rams' shoulders, he couldn't believe it!

"What do you know? Aaron caught my pass. *Wow!*"

CHAPTER 11

The Future

The Rams' bus arrived back in Rockdale to the cheers of a roaring crowd. Most everyone in town had come out to greet their first state champions.

Paul and Ann were searching for their two sons. When Aaron got off the bus, the crowd roared, "*Aaron, Aaron, Aaron!*"

Aaron looked around in disbelief. He felt shy and a little embarrassed. He'd never had so much attention before.

Paul and Ann hurried over to him. "Congratulations, son!" Paul cried. "You did great, and I'm very proud of you."

Ann didn't say a word—she hugged her son like she'd never let go.

"Hey, Mom," Aaron complained, "stop kissing me. All the guys are looking."

"Okay," Ann laughed.

When Jim got off the bus, another roar went up from the crowd. Paul looked at Ann and said, "It looks like we have *two* football stars now."

Two hours later, the Barclays sat down to dinner. First, they listened to the story of Jim's kidnapping and escape.

"You must be exhausted," Ann said. "You were up all night and then played that tough game today."

Jim grinned and nodded. "Let's put it this way, Mom—I don't think I'll have any trouble sleeping tonight."

"Well, your mom and I have some news, too," Paul said with a smile.

"What's that?" Pam asked.

Aaron stared hard at his mother and father. "I bet I know what it is," he said.

"Okay, smarty, you tell us," Ann said.

"I think you're going to tell us that you two are getting married again," Aaron said hopefully.

Paul and Ann looked at each other in

shock. "How did you know that?" Paul asked.

"All three of us knew that you guys still loved each other. We figured it was only a matter of time."

"Well, I'll be darned," was all Paul could say.

"How do you all feel about the news?" Ann asked.

"It's *great!*" they all said together.

"Now maybe we can stick around Rockdale instead of going on all those trips," Aaron added.

"Wait a minute!" Paul interrupted. "I thought you kids *enjoyed* our trips!"

Now it was Jim's turn to speak. "Think about it for a minute, Dad. We spent five days in a life raft after our boat sunk. We spent three nights in the desert when our plane crashed. On another trip, we were attacked by a grizzly bear and barely escaped a forest fire. And I'll never forget struggling through the jungle where I almost got eaten by a school of piranhas.

Somehow, I don't think *enjoy* is the right word for our trips."

Ann looked at Paul. "He has a point, you know," she said with a wink.

A week later, the city held a parade to honor their football team. And a big new sign on the outskirts of town proclaimed the Rockdale Rams as State Football Champions.

These were great days for the Barclays.

Now that the football season was over, Jim was under even more pressure to commit to a college.

Jim knew that at a major school he wouldn't play both offense and defense. The time had come to choose. And to the surprise of many, he was leaning toward playing defense. This was an important decision. In some ways, it would determine his college choice.

For several reasons, Jim was thinking of going to Penn State. First, when he visited the campus, he'd really liked it. And Penn State had probably sent more good linebackers into the National Football League than any other school.

If Jim could put on 15 to 20 pounds and improve his skills at Penn State, he might be a top draft choice for the pros. Academically, it was a fine school—so he knew he'd get a good education. And it was an eastern university. That would make it a lot easier for him to get home for frequent visits.

Lastly, Jim's best friend Tony had signed a letter of intent to play for the Nittany Lions at Penn State.

Jim told the family of his decision over dinner one evening. They were delighted.

Then Jim looked at Aaron and his sister. With a twinkle in his eye, he said, "Think of me as your role model, kiddies. *I* survived all of Dad's trips. I sure hope you two will be as lucky!"

COMPREHENSION QUESTIONS

Who and Where?

1. Which of Jim's teammates was called "the best lineman in the east"?

2. By what name was Wes Hawes known to most people?

3. Where was the state championship game played?

4. Who made the final score for Rockdale?

Remembering Details

1. How did Coach Brocko know that Jim and Tony had been in a fight?

2. Why did Jim miss most of the first half of the championship game?

3. How much did Big Louie and Snake expect to win?

4. How did Jim finally get to the state championship game?